Never Ending Journey

Colin Anderson

Ukiyoto Publishing

All global publishing rights are held by

Ukiyoto Publishing

Published in 2023

Content Copyright © Colin Anderson

ISBN 9789360163303

All rights reserved.

No part of this publication may be reproduced, transmitted, or stored in a retrieval system, in any form by any means, electronic, mechanical, photocopying, recording or otherwise, without the prior permission of the publisher.

The moral rights of the author have been asserted.

This is a work of fiction. Names, characters, businesses, places, events, locales, and incidents are either the products of the author's imagination or used in a fictitious manner. Any resemblance to actual persons, living or dead, or actual events is purely coincidental.

This book is sold subject to the condition that it shall not by way of trade or otherwise, be lent, resold, hired out or otherwise circulated, without the publisher's prior consent, in any form of binding or cover other than that in which it is published.

Contents

Preparation	1
Welcome To London	4
Consequences	9
Permanent Change	17
Nightmare	24
About the Author	31

Colin Anderson

Preparation

Dr. Georgina Taylor is typing notes into her iPad, we catch a glimpse of the calculation formulas. We hear a slight cough which catches her attention. She lets out a frustrated sigh and looks over her tinted glasses to see the person overseeing there latest project, codenamed The Door.

Georgina Taylor

(Annoyed)

What is it this time Bob? I can't let these stupid pointless… interruptions stop my valuable work.

Bob Fisher

(Angry)

Watch your tone, girl. You may be the bright star at Orion Technology. But to me your just another drain on resources, which would be served better on our project.

Georgina slowly and menacingly stands up to tower over Bob. She glares down at him.

Georgina Taylor

(Coldly)

I was personally hired by our director. I was the one who was put in charge. YOU answer to ME directly, I suggest you remember that.

She ignores him as she returns to her calculations.

Georgina Taylor

Now leave me to finish, make sure the simulation run is complete by the time I'm finished. If my formula is off by even 1 %, then all this work could be for nothing.

He scurries off as the director approaches.

David Lewis

Please excuse my interruption doctor, is everything ready.

She briefly looks up at David and smiles, then returns to her calculations.

Georgina Taylor

Bob is running the last few checks, then we're ready.

Bob begrudgingly signals that everything is ready. The both of them walk towards a large arch which lights twinkle on it like a Christmas tree. She passes her iPad to a member of her team. Who goes to a nearby terminal and begins to enter the calculations.

She looks at the arch, smiling and feeling accomplished.

David Lewis

Are you sure about this?

Georgina Taylor

I'd rather risk my life, rather than my crew.

David puts a small amount of clear liquid on her lab coat which instantaneously covers her then dissipates rapidly.

David Lewis

There, that should suffice. Your clothes will now adapt to the time period your in. The door will remain open for 48 hours only, your watch is calibrated to let you know when you should make your way back.

The arch hums to life as it comes online. The power is increased slowly as a image begins to ripple as it appears.

Bob Fisher

The calculations are set. Time period locked... England 1840, location London. All information is calibrated to your watch, it will also change appearance.

The image stops rippling and becomes clear and in high definition. She checks her watch and reads the power levels. And nods as they hold steady. She turns and gives them all a quick salute, then back to the arch, takes a deep breath and steps through.

<u>End of Chapter One</u>

Welcome To London

We see we are in London in the year 1840. The town and its roads are full of people. We are drawn to a dark alley way. A beautiful wooden door ripples into existence and it creaks open. A bright shining white light is seen as Georgina steps through. Her lab clothes change to a alluring leather corset, black trousers and a trendy hat on her head and her glasses change slightly. The door slowly closes, locks itself and dissipates. She knows its still there.

She walks out the alley and into the bustling town. She looks at her watch, now gold. She nods as it tells her the count down has begun. Three stray cats suddenly begin to follow her. She stops and kneels down to stroke them, she notices there name tags.

Georgina Taylor

(Laughing)

Hello Dodger, Raff, and little gorgeous Smokey. Aren't you just adorable.

They start to hiss and run away, as a shadow looms over her. She stands back up and turns to face a gentleman in a top hat and tails.

Man

(Posh Voice)

Excuse me peasant, out of my way

Colin Anderson

Georgina Taylor

Excuse me?

Man

I said move! Didn't your master teach you manners?

Georgina Taylor

NOBODY owns me. I am… lady Georgina Taylor.

Man

(Flabbergasted)

Oh… um… a thousand pardons my lady. Please forgive my impertinence.

He tips his top hat and bows and scurries away. She shakes her head and continues her walk. She is walking past a familiar looking home as a small girl in a dress runs into her and falls. She cowers behind her as a voice is heard screaming.

Old lady

(Shouting)

Megan Rosemary Taylor, get in the house… now!

Megan Taylor

(Whispering)

Please lady, don't let that old biddy find me.

She comes stomping up to Georgina. She spy's Megan hiding behind her, but she stops her from grabbing Megan.

Georgina Taylor

Don't you even dare, lay a finger on her… you old hag.

Old Woman

How dare you speak to your elders like that young lady. Unhand my daughter at once.

Georgina Taylor

I don't think I will. She's with me now.

Old Woman

Who are you to dictate…

Georgina Taylor

Oh shut up, you old witch. Your boring me now.

The old woman tries to use her walking stick as a weapon, and tries to hit Georgina. But she easily anticipates it and in a impressive fluid martial arts move, she takes it out of her hand. The old woman is stunned and looks on as Georgina snaps it over her knee with ease and glares emotionless at her.

Georgina Taylor

(Eerily Calm)

Not so cocky now, bitch!

The old woman runs away as her legs take her. She turns and kneels down to Megan's height.

Georgina Taylor

You alright?

Megan Taylor

Yeah, what's your name missus?

Georgina knows who this little girl is, it's her great grandmother. She knows not to let Megan know her real name.

Georgina Taylor

I'm Danielle, but you can call me Dani.

Megan Taylor

Nice to meet you... Dani.

Georgina Taylor

C'mon kid, we have to find you a place to stay.

Megan Taylor

Please don't take me back.

Georgina knows not to change things, but knows how much a hard life she had.

Georgina Taylor

Screw it, C'mon kid. Let's find you a new home.

They take a horse and carriage to the other side of town. Once they arrive, she tips the driver and they step out. The horse and carriage makes there way back to town. Georgina and Megan stand in front of a large dilapidated mansion. Megan looks at her with confusing and disgust. Georgina knows this building. It's the house where the founder of Orion Technology was born, and started the company. She hesitates, knowing the consequences of messing with events. But looking down at Megan reaffirms her decision.

Never Ending Journey

<u>End of Chapter Two</u>

Consequences

Megan is sleeping soundly on the comfy couch. Georgina is looking around the rooms. She finds a rather large cellar. She fumbles for the light switch and surprisingly it flickers into life. She is shocked to find a large copper prototype of the arch. She runs her hand over it tenderly. She receives a static as her watch reminds her not to *"Interact with important artifacts"*

She goes over to a nearby table and finds several notebooks and a diary. She is tempted to read it, but the sound of creaking stairs catches her off guard. She turns to see Megan there, yawning and rubbing off the sleep from her eyes.

Megan Taylor

I woke up and I couldn't find you. But I heard you yell... what is all this stuff?

Georgina Taylor

Its nothing for you to worry... but you can't be down here, it's dangerous. Go find a bite to eat in the kitchen.

Megan slowly teats herself away. Georgina uses her watch to scan the room. Once it stops, she presses a few buttons on it and we see a program called ARCHIVE. She taps away for a brief moment, a wide blue beam covers the entire room, and it begins to repair it. After several moments the bean recedes.

Everything looks brand new. The door closes it by itself and a heavy metal lock is heard bolting the door shut.

She again taps another few buttons on her watch and waits for a few seconds.

>Georgina Taylor
>
>Bob? You there? Can you hear me?
>
>Bob Fisher
>
>Loud and clear doctor. Everything ok?
>
>Georgina Taylor
>
>Yes, stepping through the doorway was.... Interesting to say the least.
>
>Bob Fisher
>
>Have you encountered anyone you know?
>
>Georgina Taylor
>
>I met my... great grandmother Megan...
>
>Bob Fisher
>
>(Concerned)
>
>Did she?....
>
>Georgina Taylor
>
>No, I gave a false name.
>
>David Lewis
>
>Hello doctor, its David.
>
>Georgina Taylor

Colin Anderson

Hi David, everything went well. How's the arch holding up.

David Lewis

Some fluctuations, but holding steady...

Georgina Taylor

What kind of fluctuations?

David Lewis

The temporal locks on your destination, vary every few seconds. Then return to normal.

Georgina Taylor

Decrease buffers by 1.2% that should suffice.

The com link goes silent. Suddenly an alarm sounds.

David Lewis

The buffers have failed, its going to breach.

Georgina Taylor

Remain calm, I planned for this. Decrease buffer density by 3.4... slowly. Then increase wave length by 2%... finally adjust temporal lock matrix by 5.7.

The alarm suddenly stops.

David Lewis

It's stable... for now.

Georgina Taylor

Well done, just keep an eye on it.

Megan is heard banging on the door. Georgina quickly cuts the com link, and her watch disguises itself. She hurries up the stairs and unbolts the door.

Megan Taylor

Who were you talking to down there? And what are temporal locks.

Georgina Taylor

It's just science stuff, that's all.

Megan Taylor

Your lying. I heard everything… tell me!

Georgina Taylor

I… can't. Trust me, if I did… things will change. Let's just say… I'm here on a holiday…

Megan Taylor

I don't believe you… if you don't tell me, I'll run away.

Georgina Taylor

Look kid, it's really important that I can't tell you. It would change everything… I can give you a better life, but it will take a while.

Megan Taylor

You don't know me.

Georgina Taylor

Your Megan Rosemary Taylor, your mother works in the local brothel called the Lusty maids. Your… father was a drunk and he used to visit. He met your mother, nine months later you were born… shall I go on?

Megan is dumbstruck and begins to cry a little. She nods yes.

Georgina Taylor

You work in the local coal factory, paid a pittance, left in the care of your grandmother. All she cares about is money.

Megan runs to her and hugs her tight. A slight ripple is seen moving fast across the room, then fades.

Megan Taylor

Wh… what was that.

Georgina Taylor

It's… nothing to worry about. Its getting late, best go to bed.

Megan Taylor

(Yawning)

I'm not… tired

Georgina Taylor

(Laughing)

Sure! C'mon kid, bedtime.

Georgina carries Megan to the comfy couch and lays her down gently, she puts a nearby fluffy blanket on her. She smiles happily at her, then walks back to the cellar. The door bolts gently. She goes over to the prototype arch. She pulls up the schematics on her watch and projects it on the wall.

Georgina Taylor

(To Herself)

The calculations are correct, in a small way… but the variables in this formula are all wrong. If I adjust them just a little… there.

The image ripples as the changes are made. She hooks up the clips laying beside the arch onto a generator. It sparks violently but nothing happens. She scans it and improves its design, another ripple is seen as it changes to a more impressive form. It sparks to life. Her watch beeps and the com link is reestablished.

Bob Fisher

Doctor can you hear me?

Georgina Taylor

More clearly than before.

Bob Fisher

Did you alter any of the original calculations, or anything?

Georgina Taylor

Did something change?

Bob Fisher

Yes, the arch did. To a more improved design. The formula changed too, output has improved 75%. Temporal locks holding. Time remaining 36 hours.

Colin Anderson

Georgina Taylor

Good.

Donna Green

Hello Dr.

Georgina is stunned to hear this new voice.

Georgina Taylor

Where's David?

Donna Green

Who? I have no recollection of that name.

Bob Fisher

Doctor are you ok?

Georgina Taylor

(Angry)

No I'm not FUCKING ok. Where is David, you know the director, the one who hired me and funded the project. Orion Technology? Ring any bells.

Bob Fisher

Orion Technology? That's not the name of the company, you know its Legacy Industries. Donna Green who's the director, she was the one who hired you, and funded the project.

Georgina Taylor

It's still codenamed The Doorway, right?

Bob Fisher

It was going to be, but it got renamed last minute. It's called ARCHWAY. I didn't recognize your ID code when you accessed ARCHIVE.

Georgina Taylor

What code? This doesn't make…. Oh….

Bob Fisher

You ok?

Georgina Taylor

Is there anyway I can reverse… certain things?

Bob Fisher

In theory, but it's not advisable. It could rip the fabric of space time all together. Any changes you make, alter the future. You know this.

Georgina Taylor

Oh… right, yes. I'm just….

Donna Green

Its ok doctor, a little side effect of your journey.

Georgina Taylor

Thanks Donna, best get back to it.

She ends the com link. And sits down on a recliner.

<u>End of Chapter Three</u>

Permanent Change

Georgina is fast asleep in the recliner as the sun beams directly onto her face. Megan somehow managed to unbolt the door, and gently wakes her up. Georgina jumps up awake. Megan laughs, she wipes the drool and her clothes are wrinkled but rapidly straighten. Megan sits on the recliner swinging her legs.

Megan Taylor

Sleep OK Dani?

Georgina Taylor

Eventually...

Megan Taylor

Ummm... Dani? Why does that thingy, look different. And those funny numbers look different too.

Georgina Taylor

I... can't tell you kid, if I did things would change.

Megan Taylor

(Sweetly)

Please!

Georgina Taylor

(Sighs Reluctantly)

Ok, but only a small one! You didn't go to school, yes? And work in the factory. What if I said to you that everyone can be so much better than they are.

Megan Taylor

What do you mean?

Georgina Taylor

These numbers are equations, yours to be precise. You were behind this formula. For a greater purpose.

Megan is dumbstruck. A huge terrifying rumbling is heard as a massive blue ripple like shock wave is seen. It knocks the both of them down. Georgina hits her head hard and is knocked unconscious. Megan fazes out if existence.

After a few tense moments. Georgina wakes up. She looks at the cellar in shock as it is more sophisticated and improved. She groggily gets up and makes her way to the cellar door. It slowly opens as she steadily makes her way into an impressive looking hallway. A young woman in a blue dress stands talking with a scientist, who clocks her standing there. He motions to the woman, who turns and smiles and runs to greet her. She hugs Georgina but she doesn't know who the woman is.

Woman

I'd thought I'd lost you...Georgina! I'm so happy your alright.

Georgina Taylor

Who are you, importantly where am I?

Woman

It's me... Megan... your in my home. Remember what you said to me? I can be anything I want. Well, I went back to school. Studied hard, I secured a place at a private school, passed with honors.

Georgina Taylor

So, you became a scientist. What's your field?

Megan Taylor

Same as yours, time travel!

Georgina Taylor

How... how did you know that.

Megan Taylor

Your watch spoke. Then it changed to a fancy one. You missed....

Georgina Taylor

(Panicking)

Oh no.... You still have the watch, please tell me you do!

Megan hands her the watch, and she walks quickly into the nearby study and locks the door. She presses the com link and waits.

Georgina Taylor

C'mon, pick up. Someone please pick up.

The com link is established. For a few tense moments there is silence. Then a young female voice is heard.

Never Ending Journey

Woman

Hello welcome to Memory Park. How can I help you.

Georgina Taylor

What the… isn't this Orion Technology?

Woman

You mean that second rate company next door, one moment.

The com link beeps twice and a little static is heard as it connects.

Georgina Taylor

Hello? Is anyone there?

Bob Fisher

Who is this, how did you get this link?

Georgina Taylor

Bob? Is that you?

Bob Fisher

Georgina? How this possible?

Georgina Taylor

Why is memory park…

Bob Fisher

After you…. Left, our funding dwindled. The board jumped ship and…

Georgina Taylor

The Arch? Is it still in one piece?

Bob Fisher

We had to construct a basic one, it's crude but needs must. Memory Park has it now. There the leading company in....

Georgina Taylor

(Defiantly)

Not on my watch. I maybe stuck here, but I can still help. Is ARCHIVE still available.?

Bob Fisher

That old program yes.

Georgina Taylor

Perfect. I'm bringing it up on my end. I'm going to piggy back my version into your version. It's risky but… I'm going to fix things.

Georgina taps away then hits a green button. Her watch hums, then it ramps up to an ear piercing whine. She quickly wrenches if off and the throws it onto the floor as it explodes with a loud bang. The smoke clears and we see the scientists and Megan standing there. They all look at the now destroyed watch, sparking.

Megan Taylor

Just…Why?

Georgina Taylor

Contingency plan. I just hope it worked.

Megan Taylor

Hope it was worth it.

A huge earthquake shakes the whole building. Everyone braces themselves as a massively huge ripple shock wave is seen wiping through the whole building. As it dissipates we see everything has changed again. Everything is more modernized and impressively improved. Megan looks more modern too. Her hair is short and has a lighter version of Georgina's outfit.

She finds the watch repaired and an impressive design. She picks it up and attaches itself to her. She presses the com link and it instantly connects.

Georgina Taylor

Is anyone there?

Bob Fisher

This is director Bob Fisher, Georgina you ok.

Georgina Taylor

Is everything ok? At…

Bob Fisher

Orion Technology? Even more so, actually.

Georgina Taylor

How's the arch?

Bob Fisher

Improved…

Georgina Taylor

And ARCHIVE?

Bob Fisher

Better than ever, well… everything is. Thanks to you. We're still trying to get you home. You missed your scheduled return, but there was a problem.

Georgina Taylor

What problem?

Bob Fisher

Everyone may not remember what you did, but I do. And I am eternally grateful. Those who have a… somewhat connection with you, aren't affected.

Georgina Taylor

I was only trying to give my great grandmother a better life. Is that so hard to comprehend?

Bob Fisher

I'm not saying that, am I? But please don't change things, or they may get worse. Well continue to monitor, and hopefully the temporal locks will find….

We hear a beep then a computer voice saying "Temporal locks engaged. Georgina begins to faze out of existence as Megan looks on in tears. Everything goes bright and all we hear is Megan sobbing.

<u>End of Chapter Four</u>

Nightmare

Georgina groggily wakes up to find herself handcuffed to a chair. She looks around her to see she is in a interrogation room. A female detective sits down and slaps a tablet in front of her. Georgina looks at the image. It is an alternate version of her, she has a short spiked haircut, scars, and has one robotic eye.

Georgina Taylor

That's... not me!

Detective Miller

Cut the bullshit, I know what you've done. Traitor! Your little band of resistance fighters, can't win against The League... We control everything, including your... little jaunt.

Georgina Taylor

This is insane, I'm no traitor nor do I belong here.

Detective Miller

Do you know how many times I hear that, every... single... day. Confess, and we can come to an agreement... and we'll be lenient. Refuse, and you will be executed.

There is a knock at the door and a different version of Megan walks in wearing a power suit. She nods at Georgina and then turns to scowl at the detective.

Megan Taylor

Miss Miller, do you realize who your interrogating?

Detective Miller

Yes I do, she's a traitor.

Megan Taylor

On the contrary, she is the supreme commissioner of the league. So how can be she a terrorist.

Detective Miller knows she's screwed up. She tries to back track but fails.

Detective Miller

(Pleading)

Oh wise commissioner, please have mercy.

Georgina Taylor

(Seemingly Angry)

You do realize, I could have you killed for this, but… let this be a lesson learned. NEVER pull this stunt EVER again, are we clear?

Detective Miller

As crystal supreme commissioner.

They all exit the room as the cuffs are removed from Georgina. The detective bows humbly over and over. She and Megan walk out the station and into a futuristic limo. They both get in and it takes off.

Megan Taylor

My sincere apologies commissioner, we thought you were dead.

Georgina Taylor

No… this is all wrong. Its not supposed to be like this.

Megan Taylor

Like what exactly? Everything is in order . Travelling through time is regulated, and it has a cost. You commissioner, have the honor of having the freedom to travel whenever you wish.

Georgina Taylor

So why can't we make it affordable for everyone. Surely that would solve everything.

Megan Taylor

That would go against the policy you and your father set out. To monitor time travel, to ensure it wouldn't be misused by commoners.

The limo pulls into a very expensive looking building. They both exit the limo and head through the doors which slide open. An older looking Bob Fisher hobbles towards them and struggles to bow.

Bob Fisher

Com… commissioner, it is a pleasure to see your home. May I get you anything?

Georgina Taylor

Colin Anderson

No thank you, I wish to be alone. Oh, bring me the latest report from my last venture.

Megan Taylor

I'll attend to that, it will be ready and waiting for you.

Megan courtesies and leaves. Georgina nods to bob to follow her.

Georgina Taylor

Bob? Do you recognize me?

Bob Fisher

Of course ma'am, your…

Georgina Taylor

I know that, but do you even remember me? I'd fixed everything. It was perfect… the improved temporal locks found me, and brought me… here. But everything's wrong, you… me… Megan. It's all wrong.

They enter the elevator. Bob slowly backs out, but she gestures its ok. After several minutes they exit the elevator and head into her apartment. It is extravagant and impressive. Bob mutters to himself as the door shuts. She gestures to him to sit, as she grabs the tablet off the table and looks over the results.

Bob Fisher

Ma'am? Though I appreciate your generosity it is forbidden for me to be here.

Georgina Taylor

You are my guest, you are authorized by me personally... permanently... you answer to me now ok?

Bob Fisher

Yes ma'am.

Georgina Taylor

These results, they seem right... but there not. The temporal lock variables are way off. Look.

She shows Bob the results, but he shy's away.

Bob Fisher

Ma'am please, I'm not allowed to see... personal data.

Georgina Taylor

As a personal favor to me, please Bob.

He looks at the tablet and ponders.

Bob Fisher

I agree, the variation of the lock variable is off my a huge margin. So huge, they branched out. And brought... you...

Georgina Taylor

Yes... here... its best not to mention this to anyone, not even...

We hear someone slow clapping and they turn to see Megan with two officers, pointing a gun at them.

Megan Taylor

Colin Anderson

Looks like I've found the terrorist, officers. Miller will be very pleased.

Georgina Taylor

Why Megan?

Megan Taylor

(Close to tears)

You... abandoned me... threw me aside like rubbish. I... brought you here bitch!

Bob Fisher

Miss Megan, I knew you would stoop to this.

Georgina Taylor

Wait... what? Tell me what... the FUCK is going on?

Bob Fisher

We're going to send you back, to fix things. Don't screw it up.

Things slow to a stop as things get hazy and then we see Georgina is back where she was before things changed. Megan hugs her tight with tears in her eyes.

Megan Taylor

Your alive!

Georgina Taylor

That was... a nightmare.

Megan Taylor

You just froze and you were fading in and out.

Georgina Taylor

Suspended animation. Interesting. My mind was catapulted, but my body remained here.

Megan Taylor

What happened?

Georgina Taylor

I was in a different time period, you and Bob were there. But you were... Well evil.

Georgina tenderly places her hands on Megan's cheeks and stares into her green eyes.

Georgina Taylor

I... Will... NEVER... leave you, ok! Your too important to me. Remember this... I love you with all my heart, I'll visit you everyday...

Things start to change again

About the Author

This is my very first time travel story

www.ingramcontent.com/pod-product-compliance
Lightning Source LLC
LaVergne TN
LVHW041600070526
838199LV00046B/2077